Dear Parent:
Your child's love of reading starts here!

Every child learns to read in a different way and at his or her own speed. Some go back and forth between reading levels and read favorite books again and again. Others read through each level in order. You can help your young reader improve and become more confident by encouraging his or her own interests and abilities. From books your child reads with you to the first books he or she reads alone, there are I Can Read Books for every stage of reading:

SHARED READING
Basic language, word repetition, and whimsical illustrations, ideal for sharing with your emergent reader

BEGINNING READING
Short sentences, familiar words, and simple concepts for children eager to read on their own

READING WITH HELP
Engaging stories, longer sentences, and language play for developing readers

READING ALONE
Complex plots, challenging vocabulary, and high-interest topics for the independent reader

I Can Read Books have introduced children to the joy of reading since 1957. Featuring award-winning authors and illustrators and a fabulous cast of beloved characters, I Can Read Books set the standard for beginning readers.

A lifetime of discovery begins with the magical words **"I Can Read!"**

Visit www.icanread.com for information
on enriching your child's reading experience.

Library of Congress Control Number: 2021943551
ISBN 978-0-06-297422-8 (trade bdg.)—ISBN 978-0-06-297421-1 (pbk.)

Book design by Chrisila Maida
22 23 24 25 26 LSCC 10 9 8 7 6 5 4 3 2 1
❖
First Edition

Pete the Cat's
Not So Groovy Day

by Kimberly & James Dean

HARPER
An Imprint of HarperCollinsPublishers

Pete wakes up.

He swings his legs over the bed.

Brrrrr.

The floor is cold!

Pete looks down.

Oh no!

One of his slippers is missing.

"That is not groovy," Pete says.

Pete is ready to get dressed.

He puts on his pants.

He puts on his socks.

He looks for his coolest shirt.

Oh no!

His best shirt is dirty!

Pete puts on his second-best shirt.

"This shirt is cool, too," he says.

Pete's tummy rumbles.

He is hungry!

He hopes Mom made fish!

Mom gives Pete a plate.

It is eggs!

"Eggs are not groovy," Pete says.

Pete's eggs are good.

But they are not what he wanted.

His morning is not off

to a good start.

"Time for school," Mom says.

"Get your bag, Pete.

You do not want to be late!"

Pete picks up his bag.

Oh no!

All his books fall out!

Pete looks at the floor.

It is a mess!

Pete has a lot of books.

"Hurry up, Pete," Mom says.

"The bus is here."

Pete picks up his books.

He runs outside.

But Pete is too late.

The bus is gone.

It left without him!

Pete starts to walk.

"Walking is not cool," he says.

Then Pete sees a bird.

"But that bird is cool!"

Pete gets to school.

He sits down.

"Pete, you are late,"

his teacher says.

"It is time to draw."

Now Pete is happy.

He loves to draw.

He loves to use lots of colors!

Pete opens his bag.

Oh no!

His crayons are not there!

They must be at home!

Pete draws with a pen.

He does not like his art.

It has only one color.

"This art is not groovy," he says.

In music class,

Pete plays his guitar.

His song is groovy.

Pete starts to feel better.

Oh no!

Pete's pick breaks.

He cannot play anymore.

"I do not feel cool," Pete says.

At recess,

Pete sits under a tree.

He wants to go home.

Pete does not like this day.

24

Callie sees Pete.

She sits next to him.

"You look sad," Callie says.

"What is wrong?"

Pete tells Callie about his day.

"Nothing has gone my way.

Today is not groovy," Pete says.

"Not groovy at all."

Callie smiles.

"Some days are groovy.

Some are not."

"You will be okay, Pete.

You are the coolest cat I know!"

Pete looks up.

He smiles.

"You are right, Callie!

Today is not groovy.

But I am groovy!"

"I am cooler than any bad day!"

"Way to go, Pete!" Callie says.

"Now let's go play!"

Pete and Callie
swing on the swings.

They slide

down the slide.

They kick a ball

back and forth.

Pete smiles.

He is happy.

Today is groovy after all.